THIS
BOOK BELONGS
TO

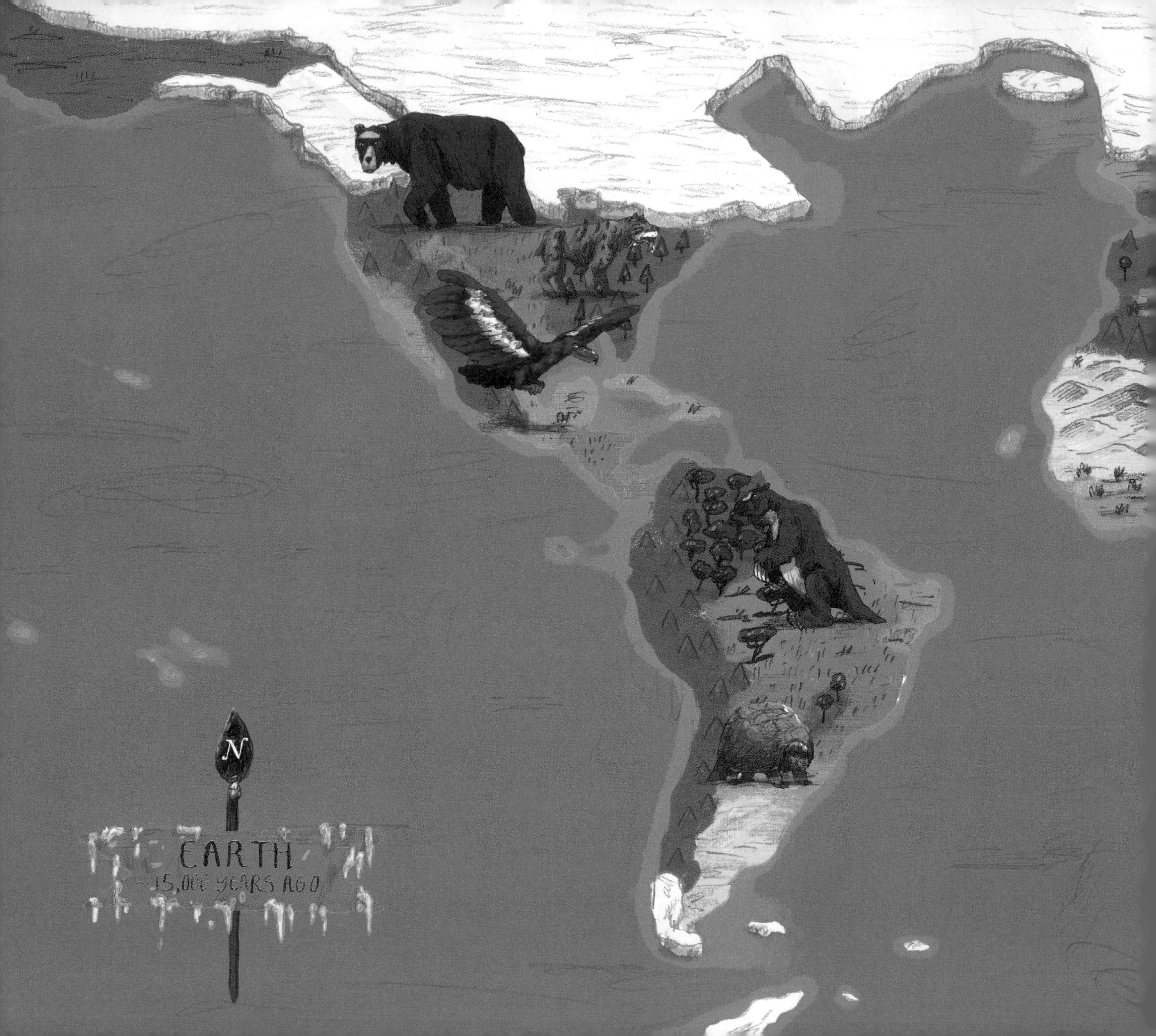
N
EARTH
~15,000 YEARS AGO

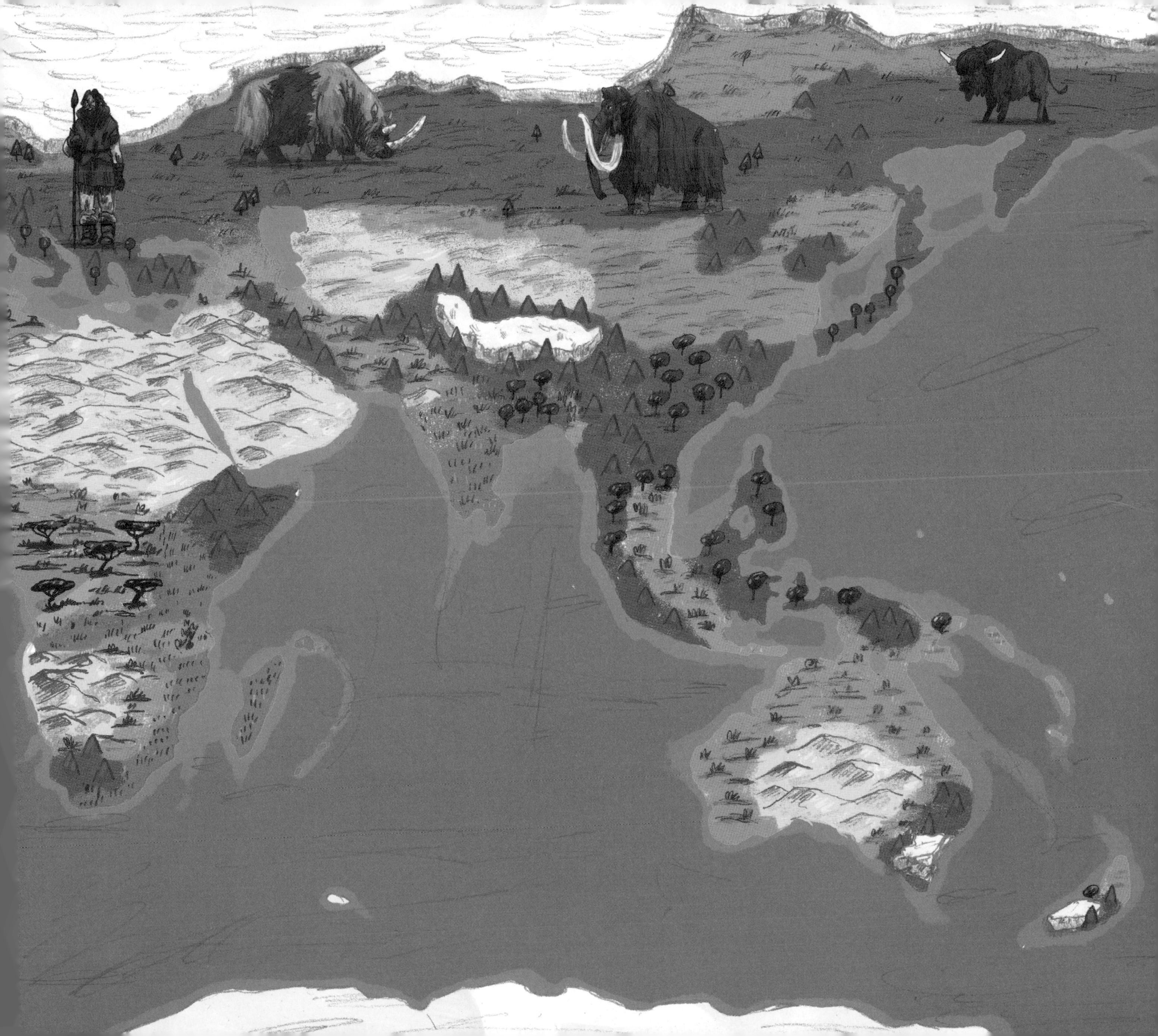

For Helen

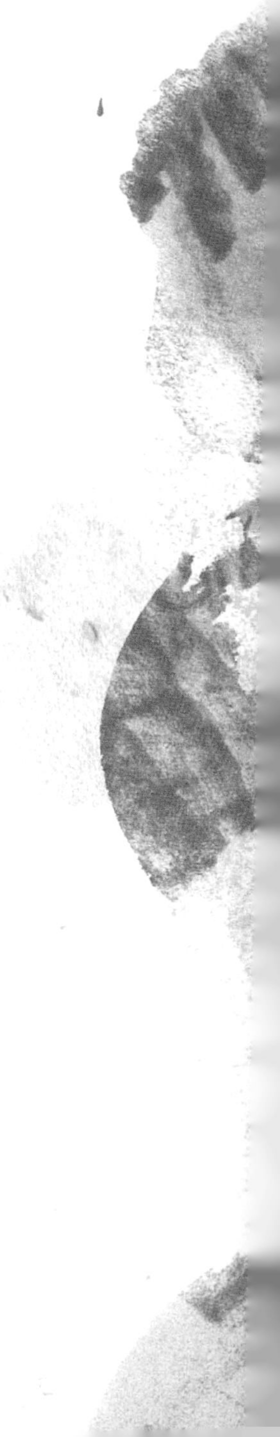

AUTHOR'S NOTE

Toby the bison lived in ice age North America, but the other Ice Age Giants lived all over the world. In reality, Toby would not have been able to finish his adventure in just one day, because the creatures in this book all lived so far apart! Toby's adventure has been told in this way so that you can enjoy a story and learn at the same time. To find the real distances and locations of the giants of the ice age, simply refer to the map at the beginning and the facts on each page.

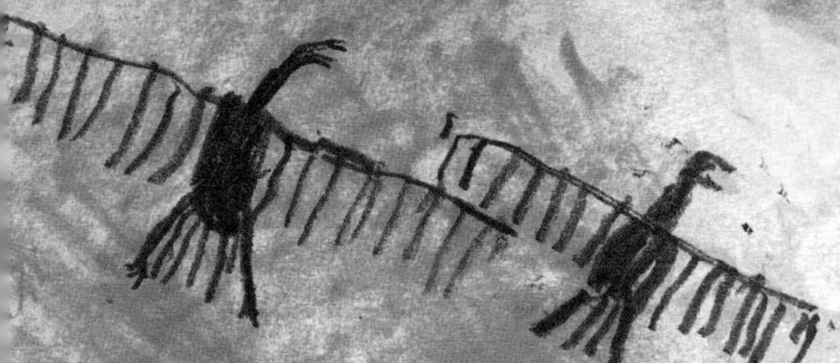

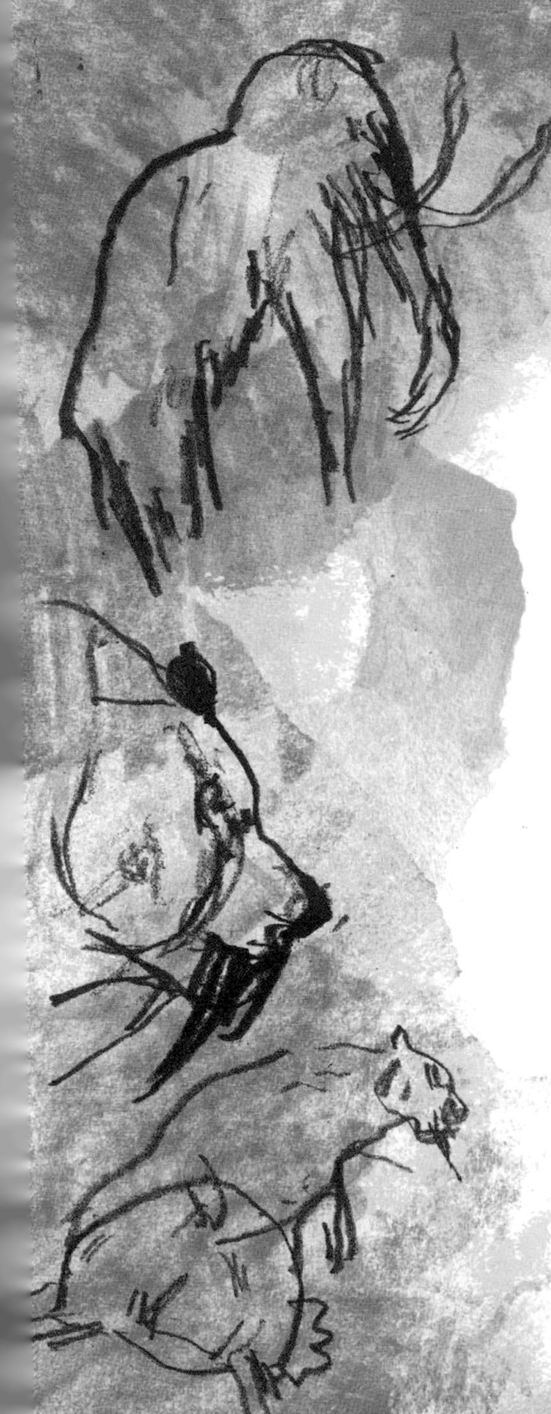

Toby and the Ice Giants

Joe Lillington

Earth has been in an ice age at various times throughout its history. During an ice age Earth is very cold and much of the world's water is frozen in huge **glaciers** in the **northern hemisphere**.

Around 20,000 years ago the world was still in the freezing depths of the ice age called **the last glacial period**, but this soon came to an end.

During this time every continent was home to gigantic animals that were well adapted to these conditions. One you might recognize is the bison.

Toby the bison lived in the ice age tundra, a vast and cold grassland. One day, he decided he wanted to go out and meet the humongous Ice Giants!

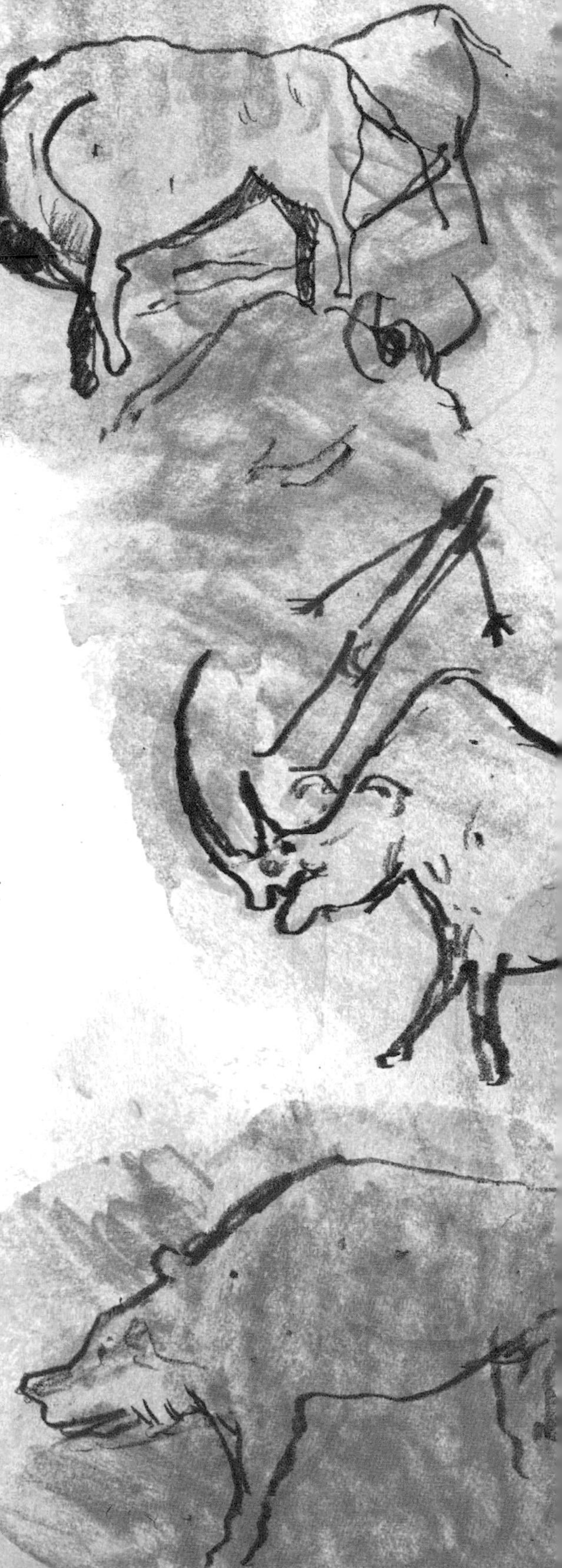

Flying Eye Books

"Don't go too far!"

"I'm big now.
I'm not scared!"
said Toby, as he
scampered away.

But before he could get very far he bumped into something very hard.

"OUCH!
Watch where
you're going!"

"Sorry!
What are you?
Why is your
horn so big?"
"I'm a WOOLLY RHINO.
My horn is for fighting with!
Do you want a FIGHT?"
"No, thanks!"
said Toby.

WOOLLY RHINOCEROS

Coelodonta antiquitatis

Size	10–12 ft long, 7 ft tall, 25–35 in long horn
Weight	6000 lb
Diet	Grasses, sedges and other plants
Habitat	Steppe tundra and polar desert in Northern Europe & Asia
Died out	8,000 years ago

Woolly rhinos were a little larger than white rhinos today and covered in a thick layer of fur to keep warm.

They had much longer horns than modern rhinos, which could grow up to 3 ft long! The woolly rhinos used their horns to fight with each other and to sweep away the winter snow to find food.

"Hello, I'm Toby Your claws are massive! Do you want to fight as well?"
"I'm a megatherium, Toby. I try not to fight all that much. I just use my claws to reach food..."

MEGATHERIUM

Megatherium americanum

Size	20 ft long, 11 ft standing
Weight	7600 lb
Diet	Leaves, twigs, fruit
Habitat	Arid desert, savannah, woodlands in South America
Died out	10,000 years ago

Megatherium were a species of ground sloth, related to modern tree sloths. They were much bigger and one of the largest mammals of their time!

They walked on all four legs but could also stand on their back legs, using their tail to balance and reach into the branches of tall trees.

Toby found his way to the sea.

"Wow, your tusks are huge! What are you?"
"We're woolly mammoths! Aren't you a bit small to be out alone?"
"I'm not small! What are you doing?"

"Being this woolly makes us very itchy. This is how we scratch the itch."

WOOLLY MAMMOTH

Mammuthus primigenius

Size	9–12 ft tall
Weight	6600–12,000 lb
Diet	Grasses, sedges and other plants
Habitat	Steppe tundra across North America, Europe and Asia
Died out	4,000 years ago

A woolly mammoth was roughly the same size as an African elephant, but its ears and tail were smaller and they had a thick coat of hair to survive in the cold ice age environment.

Woolly mammoths lived in family groups just like modern elephants, and travelled across most of the **northern hemisphere.**

Toby left the woolly mammoths and passed a strange looking creature.
"I'm Toby, I can run really fast!"

"Well I'm a Glyptodon and I'm SLOW. You would be too, if you had a heavy shell like mine!"

GLYPTODON

Glyptodon reticulatus

Size	5 ft tall
Weight	4000 lb
Diet	Grasses and plants
Habitat	North and South America
Died out	11,000 years ago

The Glyptodon was related to modern animals like anteaters and armadillos, but it was much larger.

It evolved a thick shell, like a turtle, to protect itself from **predators**. The shell could be as thick as two inches.

"Hello there, little bison. I'm a Smilodon. Don't you have any questions for me?"
"For hunting my prey..."

"Why do you have such long teeth?"
"Ahh! I think I'd better be going."

SMILODON

Smilodon fatalis

Size	3 ft tall, 6 ft long, 14 in tail
Weight	350–600 lb
Diet	Bison, giant ground sloths, possibly young mammoths
Habitat	North America and coastal South America
Died out	13,000 years ago

Smilodons were top **predators**, evolved to hunt the large animals that lived during the ice age. People often call them saber-toothed tigers even though they weren't closely related to tigers.

Smilodons were a similar size to modern lions, but were much more muscly. Their teeth were up to seven inches long, and they could open their mouth twice as wide as a lion can!

"You again, Smilodon?
Where are you going?"

"Out of my way
you big fat bear,
that's MY dinner!"

SHORT-FACED BEAR

Arctodus simus

Size	5.5 ft at shoulder, 10–11 ft standing
Weight	2200 lb
Diet	Large animal carcasses, plants, and small animal prey
Habitat	North America
Died out	10,000 years ago

Short-faced bears were the largest **pleistocene** meat eaters on land, and were larger than any bear alive today.

The short-faced bear's large size meant it had a lot of endurance, which allowed it to travel far and wide to find food from a variety of plants and animals.

"You seem like you're in a hurry..."
"Please don't eat me!"
"Don't worry! Even little bison are too big for me, I like my food to be bite-sized!"

TERATORN

Aiolornis incredibilis

Size	Wingspan 17 ft, 2.5 ft standing
Weight	50 lb
Diet	Armadillos, rodent-like mammals, possums, and capybara
Habitat	North America
Died out	10,000 years ago

The teratorn was the largest flying bird in North America. It had a wingspan of up to 17 feet, making it far larger than the wandering albatross, the bird with the largest wingspan living today at 10 ft wide.

When hunting, Teratorns would use their huge wings to glide over a wide area. Then, once they spotted their target, they would swoop down, grabbing, killing and then eating their prey without even landing!

"Who goes there?"
barked a dog.

"Just me!
And it's time
to go home!"

HUMANS

Homo sapiens

Size	Up to 5 ft 10 in
Weight	120–180 lb
Diet	Meat and some plant foods
Habitat	By this time humans had spread all over the world
Died out	Still around!

Ice age humans looked just like us, but their lifestyle was very different. They hunted and gathered while travelling all over to find food at different times of the year.

Ice age humans were very good hunters and used every part of the animal. Mammoth furs, tusks, and bones helped to create their shelters, and they were able to stitch furs together to make clothes to keep warm.

Humans had begun to domesticate dogs, which were very helpful for guarding camps and using their acute sense of smell while hunting.

"Back already Toby?
How was your big adventure?"

"Maybe I'll just stay with
you for now...

...At least until I'm a bit bigger."

BISON

Bison antiquus

Size	7 ft tall, 17 ft long, horns 3 ft tip to tip
Weight	1000 lb
Diet	Grasses, sedges, and other plants
Habitat	North America
Died out	8,000 years ago

Sometimes called the ancient bison, these animals were the direct **ancestors** of the living American bison of today.

Bison live in herds and during the ice age they lived among woolly mammoths, woolly rhinos and other **megafauna**.

After surviving until modern times, bison were almost wiped out in the 19th century because of overhunting, where huge herds of bison were killed. However, thanks to conservation efforts bison are now recovering to large numbers again.

Around 10,000 years ago, **the last glacial period** came to an end. Many of the amazing animals that had lived during this time died out.

Palaeontologists believe the cause of their extinction was partly due to the change in climate and plants. Overhunting by early humans then pushed the struggling populations to extinction.

How big are you compared to the giants of the Ice Age?
17 FT
13 FT
10 FT
6.5 FT
3 FT
YOU!
TOBY
3 ft
TERATORN
2.5 ft
17 ft wingspan
SMILODON
3 ft
GLYPTODON
5 ft
SHORT-FACED BEAR
5 ft
11 ft standing

HUMANS
Up to
5 ft 10 in
WOOLLY
RHINOCEROS
7 ft
EARLY BISON
7 ft 6 in
MEGATHERIUM
11 ft
WOOLLY
MAMMOTH
12 ft

These are some of the other amazing ice age animals that Toby didn't get to meet!

IRISH ELK
Megaloceros giganteus

GIANT TAPIR
Megatapirus augustus

MASTODON
Mammut americanum

GIANT BEAVER
Castoroides leiseyorum

MACRAUCHENIA
Macrauchenia patachonica

PROTEMNODON
Protemnodon anak

CAVE HYENA
Crocute crocuta spelaea

GENYORNIS
Genyornis newtoni

MEGALANIA
Megalania prisca

GLOSSARY

Ancestor A person from whom one is descended.

Glacier A huge area of ice that is constantly moving and changing the shape of the land surrounding it.

Northern Hemisphere The northern half of Earth.

Predator An animal that hunts and eats other animals.

Prey An animal that gets eaten.

Pleistocene The name of the time period between about 2,500,000 and 10,000 years ago.

Interglacial period A warmer time during an ice age. We are living in an interglacial period.

The last glacial period The most recent cold period in the current ice age, when Toby lived.

Palaeontologist Someone who studies extinct animals.

Megafauna Large animals.

This edition published in 2015 by Flying Eye Books,
an imprint of Nobrow Ltd. 27 Westgate Street, London E8 3RL.

Published in the US by Nobrow (US) Inc.
Printed in Poland on FSC® certified paper.

MIX
Paper from responsible sources
FSC® C001693
FSC www.fsc.org

ISBN: 978-1-913123-94-9

10 9 8 7 6 5 4 3 2 1

Order from www.flyingeyebooks.com